First published 2022 by Amazc

ISBN 9798352310566

The Gem of Destiny

Olivia Fraser-Galbraith has written various short stories with the two central characters, Custard and Muffin. As yet these are un-published and will become available in due course.

The Gem of Destiny

Custard and Muffin

And The Gem of Destiny.

Chapter 1.

Down in a secret place was a laboratory, which was trying to make everyday food come to life.

Dr. George the head scientist, or as the scientists called him "the mad scientist", was working very hard on creating a very important machine.

Dr. George was a hunch-backed man who wore a white cloak and cowboy boots. He had black hair which probably had been in a hair-tie and then it burst and his hair flung out. He had ocean-blue eyes and very thin lips. His nose looked like a witch's nose because it was very long with a few warts on it. His wrinkled skin felt like uneven rock that had been covered in rust. Dr. George was not very tall but he was indeed very small.

The mad scientist was taking a muffin and placing it into the machine which was very important. The machine was not the most safe machine in the world but he's a mad scientist so mad scientist's don't do "safe". The muffin was placed into the middle of the machine very delicately and Dr. George pressed a big red button which was the "on button", the machine started to glow and then from the top some electricity sparks started to form.

Suddenly, the machine started to shake and almost as quick as a flash the machine exploded sending the muffin out of the laboratory, the muffin flew through the air over some buildings and then landed in a house garden.

'Bye boy,' said a woman. 'I'll see you in a few days!' said the woman to her dog. 'Woof!' barked her dog, Custard. 'Don't worry, I'll not be away forever. You can entertain yourself and there's some treats in your bowl if you're hungry.' But Custard didn't want any food, he wanted to be with his mistress. He kept on barking constantly not realising that he had to let his mistress go. But she was already out the door before Custard could do any more.

Custard lay in his bed thinking about his mistress. He fell asleep for a little while and woke up but still lay in his bed.

Crash! Custard jumped out of his dog bed immediately and ran outside to see what had happened. He saw something light brown on the grass with a white muffin liner on it. Custard looked intently at the incredible site. What could it be? He wondered to himself. Something began to move, it stood up looking confused.

'It's a jolly good day today isn't it?' said the mysterious creature. Custard stood there looking speechless. 'Are you ok? You might have... Oh! I forgot to intoduce myself! Please forgive me!' said the creature looking desperate.

'My name is Muffin and I'm a muffin! What's your name?' asked Muffin politely. Custard still looking confused, told Muffin his name. 'M-m-my name is-s-s c-c-Custard.' said Custard looking frightened. 'Well hello c-c-Custard, can't wait to learn more!' said Muffin starting to get excited. 'What shall we do? Oh, there's so many things to do! What about that, no that, actually that, wait no!' said the excited muffin. 'Well...'- 'We could go to the park together, build space-ships, eat sprinkles and'- 'Wo, wo, wo. Slow down Muffin. We can't do any of those things!' said Custard. 'B-but, we can!' said Muffin. 'First off, we can't go out of this house, second, we can not build space-ships because there are no parts and third, we can NOT go to the shops and we don't have any sprinkles either!' said Custard, getting a little bit annoyed at Muffin for thinking that they can do all those things.

Just as Muffin was going to say something else a man and big hounds appeared.

The man held the hound's collars tightly, he was holding a remote in his hand and the hound's collars in the other. The hounds growled at Muffin and Custard, baring their teeth at them. The man started to run after Muffin with the remote in his hands while the hounds growled at Custard. 'Hey!' yelled a familiar voice. It was Fenton the fox, one of Custard's friends. 'NO ONE GROWLS AT MY FRIEND! ARRRGHHH!!!!!!' yelled Fenton. Fenton took a look at Muffin and blinked his eyes three times, he thought he was dreaming and when he opened his eyes again he was still in the same place he was.

Fenton jumped down from the fence he was sitting on. Fenton got Custard. 'Come on, let's go!' called Fenton to his friend. 'No wait! We need to save Muffin!' Custard said to Fenton with a determined look on his face. 'Save who?' asked Fenton. 'Never mind, just stay here Fen.' He pelted it to the front garden, he saw Muffin and jumped to where his new friend was, Muffin climbed up the dog and hung on to his red collar and off they went to where Fenton was.

Fenton pulled them up to the top of the fence, they walked along it carefully until they came to the front of the house which was connected to the road. They jumped off the fence and ran onto the road, not knowing what to do apart from run. They stayed on the road for a while, they followed Fenton, dodging cars and road hazards while they were going. 'Are we almost there yet?' asked Custard. They could hear the exhaustment in his breath. 'Almost,' said Fenton. 'Just a few kilometres to go, I think.' 'I'm hungry, very, very hungry and thirsty, very thirsty, did I mention very thirsty?' said Muffin with a dry voice. 'Why is my throat dry?' asked Muffin in surprise. 'It's dehydration, you need water!' said Fenton smartly.

Fenton was one smart fox, even though he is a fox he is still very smart. But surprisingly he is not sly. Well he is not sly to his friends, maybe bad animals or bad people. A little while later they stopped at a sewer opening. 'Here we are,' said Fenton to the others. 'The wonders of the sewers!' said Fenton with a giggle. 'You're not telling me that we have to go down there, are you?' asked Custard in a disgusted voice. 'Umm…,' said Fenton, a bit embarrassed. 'You're joking right?' asked Custard, to be sure. 'Even I know that we're going down there!' said Muffin, trying to be smart like Fenton. 'Seriously?' said Custard with a disgusted expression on his face.

Fenton sat there trying to think of what to do. He walked over to Muffin and whispered something very quietly in Muffin's ear, well not his ear but what he hears with, so his ear. Muffin nodded, his little brown face went a little bit rosy but Custard didn't notice, he was too busy looking in bushes at the side of the road.

 'Custard?' asked Fenton to his friend. 'Yes?' said Custard. 'Will we still be friends after this, no matter what?' asked Fenton, with a bit of hope in his voice. 'Yeah. Why?' asked Custard, starting to get suspicious. 'Good!' said Fenton, getting excited. He lifted up the sewer cover on the opening. 'I'm sorry to do this Cus!' said Fenton as he got in his place. And in a millisecond Custard got kicked into the sewer.

Fenton and Muffin heard a shriek from the sewers below them. Fenton jumped down with Muffin. 'What did you do that for?' said Custard , getting annoyed. 'Well...,'- 'My fur is covered in sludge, look at it! Actually, don't, that will make it worse!' said Custard. Fenton and Muffin gave each other a surprised look, they thought that Custard was mad about the journey and getting kicked into the sewer but he was mad about getting a little bit dirty.

 'Ok, follow me please!' said Fenton. Custard walked behind them closely, scared that he might be bitten by a scorpion, or break a leg, or get a deadly disease. Muffin skipped behind them, enjoying himself and singing songs and dancing around the mucky sewers.

'Now...,'- 'Ah ha! They're over here! Hounds, get 'em!' yelled a familiar voice, it was the man and the hounds that were chasing them.

'RUN!' yelled Fenton. 'Hop on, Muffin!' called Custard.

 Muffin clung on to Custard's collar very tight. 'Climb up here' called Fenton to the others. They all got away from the man and the hounds. They closed the sewer cover over the opening. 'Phew, that was a close call,' said Fenton, wiping the sweat off his forehead. 'What were you going to say Fenton?' asked Custard.

 'Now, we need to get out of the sewers and go to Maclin Island. That's what I was going to say.' 'What is Maclin Island and where?' asked Muffin. 'Maclin Island is an island and it is two-hundred and seventeen miles away and it is the location of a magical gem,' said Fenton. 'Now, follow me,' said Fenton, starting to get moving along a trail. They were in a forest, where lots of wild animals lived. Clippity-clop, clipity-clop-clipity-clop. There was a rumbling of feet nearby, it was getting louder and louder. 'Ah! Not the man and the hounds again!' said Custard in fright. 'I don't think hounds make that noise!' said Fenton.

Suddenly, a cream-coloured horse appeared, its mane was white with crinkles in it, its tail was the same as the mane, white and crinkled, like crimped hair. Its coat was cream-coloured and its eyes were blue, it stood there as if to say something.

'Bella!' cried Muffin as he jumped off Custard and hugged the cream-coloured horse. 'I've missed you so much!' said Muffin as he squeezed Bella tightly. 'Oh, this is Bella! Bella, this is Fenton and Custard!' said Muffin as he introduced each other.

'Hi, I'm Bella! And this is my best-friend, Muffin! We met about an hour ago, he was in a machine and I tried to get a man and these grey big dogs to go away but they wouldn't and then we became friends! It's so nice to meet you!' said Bella joyfully. 'You guys look as if you need a ride! Hop on!' said Bella as she got her friends on her back. 'Where are we going?' asked Bella. 'We are going to Maclin Island, so follow this trail and then when you come to the big oak-tree turn left, ok?' said Fenton. 'Ok!' said Bella.

Bella galloped off, Muffin on top of Fenton, enjoying himself. While they were on their way a few rabbits and deer passed by. They came to an oak tree a little while later, Bella turned left on to another trail that led round a meadow. The meadow was covered in flowers, butterflies, bees, and lots of other insects enjoying the sun. Crunch, crunch, crunch. They all heard something in the bushes, Bella came to a halt. They stood still for a bit until a fox came out of the bushes. It eyed Fenton and bared his teeth at him. 'Ronald!' said Fenton, glaring at Ronald, you could hear him growling under his breath. 'Fenton!' said Ronald as he glared at Fenton and bared his teeth. 'Grrrr!' growled Ronald. 'Fenny-Foo! Fenny-Foo! My silly brother Fenny-Foo!' sang Ronald, teasing Fenton. 'You know my name is Fenton! Not Fenny-Foo! Little brother! You know that! Grrrrr!' yelled Fenton strictly at his brother. 'It will always be Fenny-Foo to me brother. And nothing can change that. Fenny-Foo! Fenny-Foo! My ditsy brother Fenny-Foo!' sang Ronald again and again. 'Raggy-Ron! Raggy-Ron! My LITTLE brother Raggy-Ron! Ha ha!' sang Fenton with a giggle. 'Grrrr!' growled Ronald, he'd had enough, so pounced on his brother.

Bella gave a shriek, sending Custard and Muffin flying off. Ronald had Fenton pinned on the ground.

Muffin clinging to Custard's collar was back and so was Bella. Fenton tried to free himself but it was no use as he was still on the ground. 'Grrrr!' growled Custard at Ronald. 'NO ONE HURTS MY FRIEND!' yelled Custard at Ronald. Ronald gave no sign of attention, he was too busy growling at his brother while Fenton growled back. Custard, Bella and Muffin had decided what to do.

Custard and Muffin pounced on Ronald, Ronald got a big fright so much to make him let go of poor Fenton. Ronald gave a shriek. Bella started to rear-up and tried to hit Ronald with her front-legs when they went down. She succeeded, she hit Ronald on the back enough to scare him away. Fenton got off the ground and brushed himself off, he had a few scratches but it wasn't that bad. 'Are you ok Fen?' asked Custard, getting worried about his friend. 'Yes, I am fine, thank you. It's just a few scratches, not a big deal.' 'You were so brave out there!' complemented Bella. 'Yeah. I would never have been that brave!' said Muffin. 'Aww. Thanks.' said Fenton. 'Now, we better get going, we're far behind schedule!' said Fenton. 'And the man and the hounds might be after us as well!' added Muffin. 'Good point, Muffin,' said Fenton. 'Bella, can you keep going or do you need a break?'

They all took a fifteen minute break.

Bella galloped around the meadow, while spotting lots of insects and small animals, Muffin was prancing about singing and dancing round the meadow. Custard played with Fenton, playing with ball-like items they found in bushes.

'It's time to get going now,' said Fenton. 'Are you feeling better Bella?' asked Fenton.

'Never been better!' said Bella.

'Custard, come up onto Bella's back!' said Fenton.

'Ok,' said Custard as he hopped on Bella's back.

'What about you, Fenton, are you coming up onto Bella's back?' asked Custard to his friend.

'No, thank you. I'm going to run alongside you guys with Muffin on my back, right Muffin?' said Fenton. 'Yep! Scoop-doodle-y-doo!' said Muffin as he flipped out of a bush and landed on Fenton's back.

'Let's go!' called Fenton to the others. They both ran alongside each other, enjoying themselves very much. They ran into a few more rabbits, deer, foxs and a few more small animals. Muffin made a few jokes on the way, he made the others giggle a lot.

'That is hilarious!' said Bella with laughter in her voice. 'I love Muffin's jokes but sometimes they get a little crumby!' said Fenton with a giggle.

'We're almost there!' said Custard, delighted.

'Let's make funny accents!' suggested Fenton.

'Yes! Yes! Yes!' said Muffin excitedly.

'Ok, I'll start,' said Bella. 'It's an honour to meet you!' said Bella in a queen voice. Next up was Muffin.

'How y'all doin?' said Muffin in a cowboy voice. 'He he he!' giggled Muffin.

'Helloooo! I ammmmm Fentonnnnnnn!' said Fenton in a high voice.

'Hoy! I'm Custard, yeah!' said Custard in a very low voice. They all talked for a while.

'Fenton, I've never ever seen you fight like that before. How did you do it?' said Custard. 'Oh, well, umm…' said Fenton, not wanting to brag. Custard gave Fenton the look of truth, to see if Fenton would tell the truth. 'Oh, ok. I'll tell you the truth,' said Fenton. 'I have always known how to do it and I had to!' said Fenton. 'Come on, Fenton! We need the truth!' said Custard urgently. 'That was the truth!' said Fenton. 'Oh,' said Custard, a bit embarrassed. 'Sorry, I was a bit desperate!' said Custard, ashamed of himself. 'It's ok,' said Fenton. 'It's not like the world is about to end,' said Fenton with a laugh.

Screech, screech, screech! There was a bird above them but not just any bird, an evil bird.

'You h-hand the-the-that m-m-muffin to me!' stormed the bird. 'No!' yelled Fenton bravely. 'N-n-no!' bellowed the bird. 'Oh, you think I was just letting you go freely, well I was going easy on you until now, time for the drama to begin!' The bird swooped down to grab Muffin from Fenton's back.

'Ahh!' screeched Muffin. Even from a mile away you could see the terror on Muffin's face.

'HEY!' thundered Fenton.

'Grr!' growled Custard, furiously.

Fenton jumped up and snatched Muffin from the bird, he just got Muffin out of the bird's grasp in time.

'WHAT ARE YOU DOING!' roared the bird in anger.

'Doing what's right,' said Fenton. 'Oh yeah, I almost forgot!' said Fenton, winking at Bella. Custard got off Bella's back because she went and rubbed her tail in bird's face and then as quick as a flash bit its tail, the bird screeched in terror as zoomed off. Away it went, away and away through the air. You could hear the bird screech but it got cut off by the sea starting to roar.

'Thank you for saving me Bella!' cried Muffin happily.

'No, thank you!' said Bella, looking pleased with herself.

'Let's keep moving,' said Fenton. 'We need to keep moving or we're going to get caught by that man and those hounds!' said Fenton.

'Oh no!' said Muffin, looking worried.

'Calm down Muffin, we'll be alright,' said Fenton. 'At least hopefully!' mumbled Fenton to himself.

They kept going. They came out of the trail they were following and even out of the forest itself! They came to a dock.

Chapter 2.

'There's an island!' said Muffin in excitement. 'Well I don't think-' 'It's the island we were looking for!' said Muffin.

'Let's go!' said Custard.

'Wait, but I don't think.. oh I'll just go with them no matter if it's a good thing or a bad thing!' mumbled Fenton. They swam in the water splashing about and waving their paws, hands and hooves about.

'Ugh, this is so wet! Yuck!' said Custard in a distressed tone.

'Oh, alright, Mr Grumpy Pants!' giggled Muffin.

'Ugh, whatever?' mumbled Custard.

'Well at least it cleans you.' said Fenton, trying to break up the fight.

'Mhmm… it kinda does feel soothing!' said Custard approvingly.

'It serves you right', said Fenton. 'Yeah especially after you got so mucky in the-'

'Oh, alright, I got mucky in the sewers and… The water is nice but no more mucky things, OK?' said Custard.

'WE'RE HERE!' yelled Muffin in excitement. They travelled a long way from the shore but they were at the island. They went up the rocky shore and past a few trees. It was a nice island but they had to find the cure in time! As they all looked up they saw birds flying across the trees. 'I wonder why this island has no palm-trees? I mean one: this is an island and most of the islands I've seen have palm-trees and two: this is meant to be a tropical island!' said Muffin, making a point. 'I wonder why as well?' said Fenton.

Just then they heard a squawk nearby.

'Ahh!' yelled Muffin.

'TAKE COVER!!!!!' yelled Fenton.

'It's just me', said a toucan standing on a branch.

'Liam!' cried Bella.

'Bella?' said the toucan.

'Bella!' yelled Liam hugging the horse.

'Ok enough of the chit-chat!' said Custard impatiently. ' We need to get moving!' he said.

'Hehehehe!' giggled Liam and Bella.

'Grr… I'm being serious, you guys!' said Custard, starting to get even more impatient.

'No more messing around!' growled Custard.

They followed Custard and Fenton to the other side of the island, right to the edge.

'The-this can't be right?'said Fenton. 'Nooo!!!' yelled Fenton.

'W-what is-s it-t?' squeaked Muffin.

'We are on the wrong island!!!!'called Fenton.

'Oh no!' sighed Muffin, getting worried.

'Gosh! The man and the hounds are back!' yelled Bella.

'No please, not them again!' sobbed Muffin. Fenton went into one of his time bubbles. Fenton went for a walk around the island so he could think. He was almost on his third lap around the island when suddenly, he got a cool idea. He bolted back to the others and got out of the time bubble. He quickly whispered his plan in the other's ears.

'This way!' he said.

'Hop on!' said Bella to Muffin and Custard. Liam flew and Fenton ran, the man and the hounds behind them in confusion, they seemed to be stunned somehow.

'Go, go, go!' called Fenton to the others. 'Custard, you go first, then Liam, then Bella, Muffin and I are going to jump in together!' Custard leapt in. Bella couldn't jump in because she was a horse so instead she began rearing until her front end was in the cruiser, and then she lifted up her back end and got it in the cruiser. Liam flew to the top, hoping to get a good view. There were four stories, the top was open with an extension which was the control part, the third floor went around the cruiser with some loungers at the front and a small set of stairs down to the main floor, the middle was the main part with nice beds and seating, and underneath was below the deck, it had some food and more beds and seating. Fenton hopped on. 'And off we go!' he said proudly. They were having a great time on the cruiser. Custard was lying in the sun on the third story in a lounge. Bella was lying on a bed and Liam was playing on the top. Fenton was just about to take all their orders to the snack bar, it was just then that Fenton realised he'd forgotten Muffin!

'Oh no!' said Fenton. He was going to tell the others about it and what he should do when suddenly, he spotted something, it was a jet ski! It was quite a lucky find, if he wasn't looking that way he wouldn't have spotted it and been able to go and help Muffin. He got on the jet ski and zoomed off without telling the others. Soon, he came to the shore of the island, no Muffin to be seen. But, just then he saw something quite unpredictable, the man and the hounds with no Muffin! He looked about but still could not see Muffin. Fenton looked again and again and still nothing. Just then he had thought of a plan.

He got off the jet ski and hid it behind a rock. Then he went on to the island, searching everywhere for Muffin, still keeping distance from the hounds. He trotted through the trees and still no Muffin! 'Where could Muffin be!?' thought Fenton to himself. And then a terrible thought struck Fenton's mind, it was that Muffin got drowned in the water or he got eaten by an animal or…or…or he got poisoned by a tarantula! Ok, I have to admit Fenton's thoughts were getting a little well-out of hand, I don't think any of that happened to Muffin or could just be the case that Muffin was in the cruiser after all and just got lost. Fenton's mind was flooded with possibilities but his plan didn't seem to work. He took one last look around the small island in search of Muffin and became aware of the man and the hounds, safely avoiding them he went back to the jet ski and just before he set off again he heard a small sneeze. 'Atchoo!' sneezed a mysterious creature. 'H-h-help-me-e!' it seemed to say. Fenton, who was filled with courage to go on, went back on the island, with a determined look on his face. He wanted to see what was sneezed and he really wanted to find Muffin.

It sneezed again and again. Fenton followed the sound until he couldn't get any nearer, the creature was somewhere in this clearing. There was rustling in the bushes, Fenton got startled and jumped up a tall tree, he kept climbing until he couldn't climb anymore. He was quite lucky to have climbed that high because right next to him hanging for a branch was…

'Muffin!' yelled Fenton as he pulled Muffin up. 'What are you…'

'Shhh!' Muffin quieted him. 'Stay quiet, the man and the hounds are on the loose!' said Muffin in a hushed voice, he was whispering so quietly that if he whispered quieter you wouldn't even hear him.

'Oh…' Muffin quickly covered Fenton's mouth because the man and the hounds were coming. 'Don't dare cover my mouth, I'm whispering, they won't hear me. As I was saying… How are we going to get to the water?' whispered Fenton.

'Ah-ha! Leave that to me!' said Muffin excitedly.

'Shhh! You're gonna get us caught!' said Fenton cautiously. But Muffin was no longer listening, he was jumping through the trees.

'Come on!' whispered Muffin from a tree nearby. 'B-but what if I fall?' said Fenton cautiously.

'Oh, you'll be fine, it's fun!' said Muffin as he jumped through more and more trees. 'This is Muffin style!' celebrated Muffin through the trees, with Fenton following; right on his tail. They finally made it to the island's edge, the man and hounds not far behind.

'Ok, umm… it was this way, no that, wait, it was this way!' said Fenton as he tried to find the jet ski. They went in circles round the whole island for ages.

'Ugh, are you sure you know where it is?' said Muffin tiredly. They'd been walking for about an hour. Fenton was as worried as Muffin, he was worried that the others would realise he and Muffin were gone and panic.

'Ok I'm sure it's this way, actually this way, wait, no…'

'We've been going in circles for hours!' cried Muffin.

'I know, I know,' said Fenton, looking displeased. 'I know it is here though!' And sure enough, it was. The beautiful jet ski gleaming in the sunlight.

'It's-it's beautiful!' cried Muffin, beaming at the beautiful sight. 'We better get going then…'

'WAIT!!!! Don't leave me here on this blank island, I've been stranded here for like ever, please bring me with you!' cried a voice. Fenton and Muffin jumped. They both turned round slowly and faced a short-haired German shepherd.

'Woof!' it barked.

'Hello?' said Fenton.

'Can we help you?' asked Muffin.

'Please can you bring me with you! I've been stuck here for two years!' sobbed the dog.

'Well, umm...'

'Oh! Thank you! Thank you! Thank you!' cried the dog excitedly.

'I guess we could fit a few more animals on our jet ski,' said Fenton thoughtfully. The jet ski was quite big though. They all hopped on taking the dog with them.

'I'm Muffin!' squeaked Muffin.

'I am Fenton,' said Fenton politely. 'What is your name, if you want to share it?' said Fenton.

'Oh, how could I forget! I'm uhh... Rex!' said the dog.

'Well hello Rex, we're glad to have you!' said Fenton.

Soon they came up to the small cruiser. Bella, Liam and Custard were standing on the deck watching for the appearance of Fenton and maybe Muffin. The others screamed in joy as Fenton and Muffin got off the jet ski. Rex came off trembling.

'Uhh? Hello?' said Liam uneasily.

'Well, hello,' said Rex coldly. 'Such a surprise, you're here,' said Rex repulsively. Liam made a face at him. Rex gave Liam a dangerous look as if to say (I'm warning you don't say another word!) Rex glared at him and looked back at the others with a big fake smile on his face, it showed his grubby yellow teeth which were disgusting to look at, and if you did for too long you would probably be sick. Saliva dripped down his face and into the sea.

'Oof! Yuck!' said Muffin in a disgusted voice. They all lay on loungers above the main deck. It was only Rex who wasn't in the lounge. Liam soon got up off his lounger and started to see what Rex was up to. He went under the deck on the first floor to find Rex sneaking around in the snack bar.

'And you were going to the toilet? It's not really what I would recommend for a toilet but if you think so I guess it's ok,' said Liam suspiciously.

'Oh, don't mind good old me,'said Rex darkly.

'Oh, really? Are you even any good?' said Liam.

'Of course I am what's gotten into your evil mind- I mean uhhh... head, hehehe' said Rex.

'I-I knew it!' said Liam.

'Knew what?' asked Rex, his face blank.

'You're evil that's what I think. You don't know what I'm talking about, do you?' said Liam. Rex shook his head. He gave Liam a blank look though, it was enough to convince Liam that he wasn't evil but he still suspected something. 'What is he up to then if he isn't evil?' Liam asked himself. He had a lot more spying to do!

'This is so relaxing! I could stay here forever! Neigh!' said Bella.

'Come on guys, we're meant to be going to Maclin Island! Not staying here all day!' said Custard urgently. 'Custard, maybe let them rest. I mean we've been swimming and running so we are all a little bittle tired.'

'But still, everyone get up please!' urged Custard.

'Ok,' said Bella, getting up. Muffin got up with Custard.

'Where's Liam and-and that-that dog thing?' asked Muffin.

'I'll go and look in the beds,' said Fenton.

'Oh, they're not in the beds, they're in the toilet I think, well that's where they were going, try the snack bar as well, just in case,' said the confused Bella.

'I'll check both, but I'll check the snack bar first!' laughed Fenton. Fenton went to the beds, they weren't there, he went to the snack bar, he couldn't see them so he went to the toilet, they weren't there. 'How strange?' thought Fenton to himself. Just then when he was going to tell the others, he saw something, the fridge started to shake and talk? Fenton walked over to the fridge, he gathered up his courage to open the fridge and see what was inside. '3..., 2..., 1..., OPEN!' yelled Fenton. He opened the fridge and to his greatest surprise he found Liam tucked inside. 'Liam!?' said the surprised Fenton. 'How could it have been you, I thought it was a FRIDGE MONSTER! I did not have the slightest idea it was you. Anyway, what are you doing in the fridge?' said Fenton.

'P-p-t-u-uhh... I-I uhh... I think it's going to be a clear sky tonight!' said Liam trying to change the subject to something else.

'Yeah, now spill!' said Fenton.

'Please I'll tell you later in private now shhh!' said Liam urgently. 'B-but...' 'Shh!'

'Alright, alright!' whispered Fenton. 'Who's watching us?' asked Fenton. Liam pointed with his feather upwards. And, in the shadows on the ceiling was a figure.

It was the evening, they'd been travelling by boat for hours and hours. Custard, Bella and Muffin were fast asleep. Back downstairs the two of them were staring at the figure. They couldn't make out what it was or the shape of its body but Fenton could make out its eyes, tiny black holes with a glint of reflection. They could catch a glimpse of it and then it just disappeared into thin air, Fenton and Liam could not figure out what had just happened. Soon they got some snacks and drinks ready for the interesting event and brought it up to the others.

'Wow! That's even scary for me!' said Bella.

'What if-if it-t comes again!' squeaked the frightened Muffin.

'Don't worry the almighty Custard will protect you!' bragged Custard. The others giggled because this seemed to be a joke for them but not for Custard. After they're yummy snack they went to the beds. They were all tired but Custard was grumpy because he was woken up from a very good dream of him being an almighty hero.

There were only three beds there for them to share. Bella slept with Liam, the next bed was big enough for three so Custard, Fenton and Muffin shared one, so that leaves just one more small bed and it was for Rex who finally turned up. Everyone was sleeping apart from Fenton, he was wide awake, he kept going back to think about the figure, he knew something was there that shouldn't have been.

Chapter 3.

In the middle of the night Fenton heard a crash. He sat up looking so tired that around his eyes were black. He gave a big yawn and got up without making a noise. He went to the snack bar and hid behind the counter. Soon he gave up and was going to go back to bed when suddenly, he saw a figure walking towards the counter, he held his breath and tried to hide in the shadows. The figure looked like a person but very small. It went to the fridge and grabbed something that Fenton could only catch a glimpse of, it was something very, very small with red, white and silver on it. Before the figure went to leave it stopped, it turned its head so slowly it was like Fenton was in a horror movie, it gave Fenton a sharp look and said something unbelievable;

 'I would watch out if I were you, and take your little friends away, especially that talking Muffin, you have until sunset on the last day of this week or else… something is coming for you and your friends!' said the creature sharply, then it turned and walked away.

 'Some things are coming for us,' said Fenton. 'Some things are coming for us, just what though?' repeated Fenton again and again. He went back to bed, his head spinning. Hopefully he will get a good night's sleep. He woke up early in the morning, remembering the nightmare he had; it was that the figure came at the dead of night and took all his friends and decided he should be a slave. The one thing Fenton hated most was being a slave or even the word "slave". He told the others about what the figure said and they were all panicking; 'W-what are we going to do!' wailed Bella.

'It's after us! It's going to eat us up for dinner!' sobbed the over exaggerating Muffin.

'What am I going to do! There's no brushes in dungeons, is there!?' cried Custard.

'I knew we were being followed, so I rest my case!' said Liam. But for some reason Rex wasn't that bothered about it all.

'I mean it's just words, no harm,' said Rex calmly. Liam's face went red.

'YOU THINK THAT THIS IS NORMAL!' 'Well it's just-' 'THIS IS NOT NORMAL, THIS IS A TRAGEDY! Oh, and don't go around saying "Well it's just words," in that silly voice of your's, ugh!' croaked Liam.

'Ok, ok calm down, calm down,' said Fenton trying to break the fight.

'Oh don't go around telling me to calm down! Tell HIM to calm down!' growled Liam viciously. Later on they all got some breakfast, Bella wanted to go swimming after breakfast but Fenton denied it because they had to keep moving. Bella explained she was a fast swimmer and said she could swim double the boat's high speed. She was allowed to go in to her delight. She did a smooth summersault into the water and gave a big splash. They kept on moving, half way through the journey, they stopped and saw something, they were quite far out from the mainland so it was quite hard to see but there was a huge banner saying; Jermi's Zoo Opening Day! All are welcome! Any animals you want to get rid of bring here! Enjoy! 'That is-is outrageous how-how could they do such a horrible thing "Get rid of animals" ugh!' moaned Bella.

'Maybe it's not such a bad thing?' added Rex.

'Not a bad thing! NOT A BAD THING! It's a TERRIBLE THING! I've read about it, it says to the public, that they re-energise the animals and heal them to go out to the wild, but I heard them say once an animal comes in there never comes out! Even worse they go to the WILD and catch FULL-HEALTH animals and keep them at that-that ANIMAL-PRISON! They also find a baby animal with its mum, capture the mum and leave the baby there to die!' cried Bella furiously.

'Oh no, that sounds scary!' sobbed the scared Muffin. They kept going. They were all up to different things; Bella was swimming in the water, talking to fish and dolphins, Custard was sun-bathing on a lounger, Liam was patrolling by flying above the small cruiser and watching, Muffin was in a bed looking out at the sea, Fenton was using a map to navigate to Maclin Island and Rex was sneaking around the snack bar as always. It was a lovely day, the sun was shining and it was so hot that if you had no suncream you would burn to a crisp! Fenton navigated the cruiser in and out of islands. They all wanted to stop for a break.

'Pl-please!' squeaked Muffin.

'No, sorry,' said Fenton.

'Pretty please!' squeaked Muffin again.

'I said no, sorry!' repeated Fenton.

'What if I ask really nicely, please?' chirped Muffin.

'Oh, uhhh… alright! Not for long though, a very short break and we're back, OK?' said Fenton to make sure Muffin was listening.

'Ok, blah, blah, blah! Now let's have some fun!' said Muffin. They came to a very small island. There were some blankets they brought out and set them on the hard rocks.

'Is this ok?' asked Bella.

'It is very nice! Don't you think!?' squealed Muffin comfortably. Liam wanted to fly around the island. Muffin lay down, thinking of the adventure they were going to have. Custard sometimes thought that Muffin didn't realise the dangers they were facing. Muffin didn't realise that if they didn't find the gem in time he would no longer be alive. They made a camp-fire in the evening.

'I am going to sleep here for the night,' said Fenton.

'Oh, cool!' squealed Muffin excitedly.

'Do you mean that we are staying here for the night!?' said Custard.

'Well, you can stay in the-'

'Yes! See ya' guys!' said Custard as he skipped happily back to the boat. Custard was not a "Camping dude" he liked modern things, not old things or even getting a tiny bit dirty, the one thing Custard hated the most was getting dirty. When it came to eight o'clock they all agreed to go to bed except for Fenton who said he was going to keep watch for a bit. Soon after, Fenton went to bed, he lay on a blanket, closed his eyes and fell asleep. Muffin was the only one awake. He sat up on the blanket he was lying on and shivered. It was a dark, dark night and a very cold night as well. Muffin decided to go to the boat and sleep with Custard on the bed. He left Fenton and his blanket on the rocks and leapt onto the cruiser. He felt the soft and warm quilt on the bed and fell asleep almost instantly.

It was now morning. The sun shone down on the cruiser and reflected off the glass. It was such a lovely day! Custard liked to have a long lie, but Muffin thought a bit differently. Muffin jumped up off the bed like a rocket. He was in a very good mood. He saw Fenton outside, he was clearing up the blankets until Bella said;

'Why don't we have breakfast outside?' suggested Bella.

'Sorry Bella, we need to have breakfast on the boat because we don't have much time,' said Fenton. Bella trotted around the patch of land for a bit while Fenton cleared up the blankets. Muffin wanted to play with Custard so badly that he started to jump up and down on Custard's side. It wouldn't feel painful unless you were a mouse but if Muffin jumped on you, it would feel like a little feather tickling you. Custard finally got up. He gave a yawn and a big stretch before realising that it was morning.

'Let's play! Let's play!' cheered Muffin.

'Not now, I mean-'

'Yes! Yes! Yes!' laughed Muffin.

'Oh no! I need to clean my paws, brush my teeth, brush my fur, clean my ears, stroke my tail, wipe my nose and-and-'

'Oh, shh! Stop making such a fuss!' said Muffin had attempted to drag Custard out of the bed and get him to play with him but it didn't work because Muffin was a muffin.

'Mhmm, fine!' said Custard. 'But I am not playing horsey!' assured Custard.

'Ok, I have another fun game!' said Muffin gleefully. Custard got up, he brushed his teeth and was about to have a bath before Muffin stopped him.

'No baths, you'll get dirty out here so it's better to have a wash afterwards,' suggested Muffin.

'Uhh, ok?' said Custard. 'Now what are we playing?' he asked Muffin.

'You'll see!' said Muffin. Muffin cleared his throat and began talking; 'The new game we are going to play is called er- zooming in the sun!' stated Muffin.

'This is new!' thought Custard to himself.

'Ok now just let me on your back and I'll tell you the rest!' said Muffin. Custard let Muffin on his back not knowing that it was a trick.

'Now, yee-ha!' yelled Muffin.

'NOO!' groaned Custard. Muffin yanked Custard's collar and Custard sped away. Soon Muffin slipped off and he turned Custard the other way and pointed at something as a distraction to get back on his back. He yanked the collar again and Custard sped off once more. Later they got back to the cruiser, Custard as dirty as ever! They found Fenton looking very worried.

'Where have you two been! We need to go!' said a worried Fenton.

'Well Muffin here-' started Custard.

'Got Custard to go on a walk with him!' finished Muffin. Muffin winked at Custard and Custard gave him a what-did-you-do-that-for look. Muffin shrugged. They all went to the cruiser. Custard went to take a nice warm bath, Bella went to sunbathe and Liam was about to go on patrol when suddenly he realised;

'We've forgotten breakfast!' stated Liam.

'We'll have it on here!' added Fenton. They got all their breakfast supplies and started to eat. They were full afterwards. Custard had his bread, butter and fruit after his bath. While the others had pancakes and sausages. They had lots of fun and games and personal time as well. Bella sat in the third floor and read a magazine, Liam played catch with a ball of seaweed with some dolphins, Muffin was sitting on a bed in the lounge and was watching dolphins out of the window, Custard was now lying in the sun with Bella and Fenton was trying to understand the map.

'I'm pretty sure Maclin Island is here but it doesn't show on the map!' thought Fenton. He was getting more and more frustrated. They all stopped enjoying themselves pretty quickly; the water was getting colder and colder, Liam couldn't stand it anymore, the dolphins didn't like it either and they said they had to go, dark clouds were flooding across the sky, Bella didn't enjoy the cold either. Custard hated the cold, he ran in muttering to himself. Poor Muffin was hiding in the blanket, shivering and shaking, he soon got accompanied by Custard and Bella.

Fenton was still staring hard into the map, suddenly, the wind picked up and headed North and took the map with it.

'No!' cried Fenton. He stared at the map zooming away. Just then Muffin came out shivering, he saw the map and hesitated, it took a second for him to blow away because he was so light.

'Ahh! Help me!' cried Muffin as he blew away. He prayed the wind would stop, eventually it did but not in the way he wanted it to. The wind stopped so quickly that Muffin fell from the air and landed in the sea. Muffin disappeared into the sea. Just then, Bella and Custard came out.

'What's happened?!' barked Custard.

'Well um...-' croaked Fenton. Poor Fenton had no idea what to say. Custard gave him the look of suspicion.

'Muffin blew away in the wind!' Fenton blurted out.

'Aha! The look always works!' cheered Custard. The others looked at him.

'I mean uhh... oh no! Poor Muffin!' said Custard unconvincingly. They all gave each other exchanged looks. They stood there for a while until a lightning bolt shot down on an island nearby. They all jumped in fear and surprise.

'In the boat!' yelled Fenton as he took charge. They all hurried in. They went to the snack bar. They all sat down and stared at the floor. By lunchtime no-one noticed that Rex was not there. But they were too busy eating. They heard footsteps coming down the stairs, it was Rex, looking as blank as usual. The others didn't trust Rex apart from Fenton. They all disliked him, they were very suspicious of his blank expression.

'Good morning, Rex,' said Fenton politely. Rex looked at them and said nothing. He went to the fridge, grabbed a glass of what looked like grubs and fled up the stairs.

'Interesting,' said Custard with a cunning look on his face. 'Let's follow him!' he suggested. 'Who's with me?'.

'I am!' said Liam, looking desperate and excited.

'Me too!' added Bella. By this time Fenton wasn't listening.

'I'm just uhh… Going to the toilet!' said Custard.

'Me too!' said Liam.

'Me three!' added Bella. They all went quietly up the stairs and looked around for Rex. Soon Liam spotted him going to the toilet door and shutting it.

'Uhh! He's in the toilet!' groaned Custard.

'Well here's a key-hole we can look through!' said Liam. Liam peered through the hole, he could not believe his eyes. Liam took his eyes away from the hole. He stared into the distance.

'What did you see?' asked Bella. Liam looked at her, took a deep breath and started to talk;

'-so that's what I saw!' said Liam.

'Wow!' called Bella.

'Oh, my, gosh! I mean uhh… I knew it, I knew it! I knew what he was up to! I knew it!' said Custard proudly. The others giggled.

'Keep it a secret though!' stated Liam. They promised to keep a secret. Just then, the bathroom lock started to fiddle.

'Someone's coming! Run!' whispered Custard. Bella and Custard made a run for it. Instead Liam flew upwards, he hid in the shadows, still letting in a little bit of light to see what was happening. And to his utter amazement, what had come out of the door was not Rex, it was a muffin. Liam held his breath, or else he would have screamed. The muffin looked quite wet leaving drips on the floor. He knew that this was a trick. He ran to tell the others but before he knew it the fake Muffin was there. They were all hugging Muffin.

'Muffin's back!' cried Bella happily.

'I think I can see that,' mumbled Liam. Liam stared at the Muffin in utter disgust. The Muffin glared at him and then gave a sly smile back to the others. Liam knew someone he could trust but would they believe him? He went to the lounge with Fenton. Fenton was quite happy to get away from Muffin because he was suspicious of him too.

'What's up?' asked Fenton.

'Well, you might think I'm crazy but I kinda-' Just then Bella burst into the room.

'Hurry! Hide me! Muffin, Custard and I are playing hide and seek! Help! Oh no, here he comes! Muffin's a very good seeker! Now, hide me!' said Bella in a hushed voice.

'Uhh... I'll tell you later,' sighed Liam. He walked away, muttering to himself. Later, Liam saw Muffin act a little suspicious. He hid behind a cabinet and watched the Muffin. The Muffin brought a cauldron from the bathroom and placed it on a counter, he grabbed a few ingredients from the fridge and placed them into the cauldron, he added a mixture of dark-green liquid into the cauldron, it sizzled, bubbles were pouring out of the cauldron and onto surfaces. The

Muffin grabbed a spoon and started to mix it up. 'Almost perfect. Just a few more ingredients and then the fun will begin! He he he!' muttered the Muffin.

'HUH?!' screamed Liam. The Muffin stopped dead in its tracks. It turned around to look at Liam.

'Well, well, well! Who do we have here?' laughed the Muffin.

'I knew it! I knew you were trouble!' growled Liam.

'I am trouble, and there's nothing you can do about it!' said Muffin.

'Oh, you'll see, I'm on to you!' squawked Liam, furiously. The Muffin stalked away. Liam was going to go to Fenton, when Fenton came to him and said,

'Oh, so glad you are here. Now, what were you going to tell me?'

'Huh? Oh, yeah! Umm, this might sound crazy but...' (Liam took a deep breath) '...that muffin is not Muffin, I think it is Rex,' said Liam. Fenton stared at him.

'I know what you mean! He didn't know who I was and said "ooohhhh! I love Ronald so much!" and who's standing right next to him, me! He doesn't listen to me and ignores me!' cried Fenton.

'Ohh! I have something I need to tell you,' said Liam.

'What's up?' said Fenton. 'Well, you see, I saw Rex go into the bathroom. I was suspicious so I peeped through the keyhole and lucky I did because I saw tons and tons of ingredients and a cauldon. Rex was using a spoon to mix and then he looked at me, I heard the key turning on the door and I jumped into the shadows and guess who came out-'

'Who? Wait, was it Ronald?' said Fenton.

'No, it was Muffin! But not the regular Muffin we know, an evil Muffin!"said Liam. Fenton stood there, looking stunned, he opened his mouth to say something but nothing came out. Soon he could talk again and said; 'We've got some serious investigating to do,' he said. They both came down to the snack bar and found the muffin mixing something.

'What're you up to?' said Liam gleefully.

'None of your business!' snapped the muffin.

'Well, I'm sure the least you could do is to tell what you're up to,' said Fenton pleasantly.

'I'm pretty sure I told you that it's none of your business!' growled Muffin.

'You did but we are not listening,' said Liam.

'Go away!' yelled the muffin.

'No, I think I'll just stay here,' said Liam with a slight smile on his face.

'Anyways, what are you up to?' asked Liam.

'Nothing! GO AWAY!' screamed the muffin.

'Why!?' snapped Liam.

'Ok, ok, you win Muffin, we'll go away now,' said Fenton calmly with a slight look at Liam. Liam nodded and walked away with him.

'Yeah, go cry to your mummy,' giggled Muffin. Liam had had enough;

'Oh, you think that's funny!' snapped Liam. 'Well, I'll have you know I used to fight other birds!' screamed Liam furiously. Muffin stared at him. Liam was so mad that he went and grabbed the cauldron and smashed it on the floor with everything still in it. The muffin screamed in fury and ran away.

'At least he can't make up his evil plans in that thing now!' said Fenton. 'It felt great, but I mean my body just did it-' (Liam looked down at his tummy) '-I couldn't control it!' lied Liam. Fenton giggled.

'Nice, but still, it wasn't real Muffin!' repeated Liam over and over.

'Ok, I believe you but we need to convince the others!' said Fenton.

'I know! We could get them one at a time to see what Muffin's up to and then they'll believe us!' said Liam thoughtfully.

'Yes!' cried Fenton.

Chapter 4.

The next morning Liam woke-up with a fright. He had had a terrible dream. He let out a big sob of sadness and turned over in the bed to realise that it was just a dream. Bella was already up, she was in the snack bar watching television. Fenton and Muffin were the only ones in bed. Custard was doing his daily bathroom routine as usual. Liam stretched out his wings and sighed. Fenton meanwhile was talking in his sleep. Liam went over to him and gave the blanket a shake, enough to wake-up Fenton. Fenton and Liam went to the snack bar and discussed their plan from the previous night while they ate. After they cleared up the plates they went to the bathroom to brush their teeth. They went in forgetting about Custard and his daily wash and saw something very interesting that was a bit gross. They came and found Custard singing and dancing in the shower with the water running and bubbles all over him. Custard screamed like a girl. The others giggled.

'Don't you respect a dog's privacy!?' he snapped.

'Oh Custard, there hasn't been a murder. But, can you do that scream thing again, you sound like a female pig!' said Liam with great interest. Custard shot him a you-know-what-the-answer-is look and said;

'Liam! I will have you know that-that-' 'You scream like a pig!'.

'Oh shh! I just scream like that and I can't help it!' said Custard, a bit embarrassed.

'Anyway, get out, I'm trying to do something here!' said Custard.

'It's just brushing our teeth and you take ages in there please!' begged Liam.

'Oh, ok. But ultra quick!' said Custard reassuringly. Fenton and Liam brushed their teeth and fled out the door before Custard could shove them away. Fenton and Liam were so focussed on playing with dolphins that they forgot all about their plan!

'Nice Oscar! But I'm still ahead!' said Liam.

'Ooohhh! Nice move! A bummer it didn't work!' said Liam. There were lots of oohs and aahs.

'Ooh! Ten nil to me!' hoorayed Liam happily. An hour or so later it was fifteen to ten to Oscar, Liam was quite surprised that Oscar was ahead of him.

'Why don't we play teams?' suggested Oscar happily.

'Oh, but there's an odd number and not enough players!' said Liam sadly.

'I know just what to do!' said Oscar. He made a sort of loud squeak noise and then out of nowhere came about nine dolphins.

'Nice!' said Liam, impressed.

'Oh, but there's still an odd number!' said Fenton.

'Oh, that's because Benjamin here is the commentator, isn't that right Benjamin?' said Oscar looking at Benjamin.

'Yes, it is Oscar,' said Benjamin. Benjamin was a rather skinny dolphin with lots of seaweed wrapped around him, he had brown eyes and a speckled muzzle. He swam to the bottom of the water slide of the cruiser and sat there watching the teaming. It was all very chaotic so Fenton took charge.

'Ok, stand in a line in front of me and I'll number you. Oscar is team captain for team No.1 and Liam is team captain of team No.2. Ok, got that?' (There was a big yep from all the dolphins)

'Good, now Chad No.1, Calum No.2, Freya No.1, Billy, No.2, Lavender, No.1, o-o-Olive No.1- I mean uhh… two No.2!' said Fenton. He numbered another four including himself. He was on team No.1 while Olive was on team No.2. Fenton liked Olive so he tried his best to impress her. The game of seaweed throw had begun. Seaweed throw was like you had a ball of seaweed and you had two stands with a hoop on the end, you pass the seaweed to your teammate but you can only move five paces with the seaweed ball but if you move anymore the other team gets a penalty, the rest of the rules are in the rule book. Oscar's team renamed their team to the Splashers while Liam's team renamed his team to the Swimmers. Another dolphin came to be the referee and then the game came into action.

'Ok, here we go! We got the throw up, who's gonna get it? Who's gonna get it? And ohh! It comes to the Swimmers! Great pass to Olive and to Rachel and ooh! Interception! Oscar gets his fins on the ball and makes a great move to pass to Chad. Chad passes to Fenton. Fenton moves four paces and passes to Freya, Freya makes a move to the goalposts and shoots. Ohh! Saved by Adam! Come on Freya you got this! I mean come on Splashers!'

'Ok, we need the triangle formation and then Chad you shoot, Freya pass to Chad, Fenton, I'll pass to you and you pass to Freya!' said Oscar in the team huddle. They came back out and played again.

'Ok back from water break! Now the throw! And it's its'! Oww. The Swimmers. Ok, tight pass to Olive from Calumn. Olive passes to Rachel and ohh! Rachel scores! She got past Zed! One nil to Swimmers. Ok here we go! The throw again, and the Splashers get it! Oscar passes to Fenton, Fenton passes to Freya and Freya passes to Chad- FOUL! Penalty for the Splashers and yellow card to Daren! If he gets another yellow card he's out of the game! Chad takes the Splashers penalty and he scores! Well done Splashers! Whoo hoo!' Splashers got another goal and Swimmers got another three goals.

'Ok, half-time break!' called Ben who was cheering off the Splashers.

I can't believe Daren did that!' commented Lavender.

'I know, I can't believe he shoved Chad out of the way and thinks it's fine!' growled Oscar furiously.

'Can we get those energy bars now?' asked Freya hungrily.

'Oh! Sure!' said Fenton as he went up to the cruiser and went to the snack bar to get some energy bars and energy drinks. On the way he saw Muffin watching TV but he was watching criminal things on it. Fenton stopped in his tracks and watched Muffin watch how-to videos of criminal activity. Fenton stared at the TV and then at Muffin who was taking notes on a notepad. Fenton peered over the chair to get a closer look but it was way too close and he couldn't risk getting caught so he tiptoed back outside and sat on the edge of a fold-out waterproof mat that lay on the water which was connected to the cruiser.

The dolphins sat with him eating and drinking their energy bars and drinks. After about ten minutes Benjamin called them back to the game to play the second half of the game. The second half was quite interesting, there were close calls and gladly no-one got injured and there were no more fouls. The game ended at one o'clock in the afternoon the score was 22-21 so the Swimmers won. They all shook each other's fins, paws and feathers and then the dolphins got ready to go, said goodbye and off they went. After the game of seaweed throw they were all in a very good mood. Fenton and Liam went to the snack bar to get lunch and ran into an excited Bella on the way.

'What's up, Bella?' asked Fenton.

'You ok?' asked Liam. Custard ran up to them and looked at Bella nervously.

'Have you been poisoned?!' asked Custard cautiously.

'Of course not! I was just playing with Muffin and he said we could play hide and seek on an island!' squealed Bella joyfully.

'And? What's exciting about that?' said Custard. Bella gave him a nasty look and said;

'Well, Muffin's our friend and it's exciting to play with him!' said Bella.

'Actually, that's not Muffin,' Liam blurted out without thinking.

'Ahem,' said Fenton. 'Oh, sorry,' whispered Liam. They watched Bella give a shriek of horror;

'What d'you mean that's not Muffin? THAT IS MUFFIN ALRIGHT! WHAT ARE YOU SAYING!?' shrieked Bella.

'Just listen you dustbin! Your head is full of lullabies and not what is in the real world!' snapped Custard.

'I'm going to the snack bar, and NO-ONES TO FOLLOW!' said Bella furiously as she left the room.

'Well…' started Fenton. 'Ugh, she's such a baby! She can't even think for one second what's in the real world! Her head's full of baby toys!' moaned Custard.

'She is NOT!' protested Liam. 'Uhh… she is!' 'SHE IS NOT!'

'Oh ok, you win, you win, you're right she's not a baby, she's a baby DUSTBIN!' said Custard.

'Oh, Custard, stop it!' said Fenton.

'Ugh, whatever,' said Custard disapprovingly.

'I am going to go and see Bella,' said Liam as he went down to the snack bar. 'Bella?' said Liam softly.

'Oh, Liam!' sniffed Bella. 'I wish Muffin was here,' she cried.

'I know, I know,' said Liam. 'But we could-'

'What are we going to do without him?' sobbed Bella.

'I know but- wait, how do you know that that's not the real Muffin?' asked Liam in surprise.

'Well, I found out last night because he asked me my favourite colour and I asked him his and he said BLACK. Black is Muffin's least favourite colour, because Muffin's favourite colour is orange. So by then I knew that was NOT Muffin!' explained Bella.

'Wow!' said Liam. They both talked for a bit and then left the snack bar and went to the third floor to the lounges. They gazed up at the stars, pointing at constellations, and wishing every time a shooting star went by. At about nine o'clock they both went up to bed. They both had great sleep and good dreams.

Chapter 5.

In the morning the sun shone on the glass and reflected back. They all stretched and got up. Custard taking a bath as usual. Fenton made the others breakfast and went to the top of the cruiser to steer. Eventually, he saw an island up ahead. Maybe this could be Maclin Island! Fenton thought to himself. The boat sped along the water, creating big waves behind them. On the way a few big waves came and Fenton steered out of there way. By about eleven o'clock they came to the island. Bella leaped out onto the island before anyone else.

'Let's set up some tents and-and-'

'Hold on Bella, this is not a camping trip we are here to try and find the gem-'

'And Muffin!' added Bella.

'Yes, and Muffin,' said Fenton. Fenton found a big bag and filled it with food, water, blankets, first aid kit and a small bag. They started to hike around the little island in search of the gem and Muffin. They were there for about an hour until they found something interesting;

'A golden feather?' said Custard.

'A golden feather!' said Bella excitedly.

'What's the help of a golden feather?' asked Custard dully.

'Don't you know?' (Custard shook his head) 'A golden feather is good luck!' sighed Bella happily.

'Ugh, good luck, don't you mean good yuck?!' sneered Custard. Bella glared at him. They kept on hiking until they found a hole in the ground;

'A hole?' said Fenton.

'Wonder what's in there?' said Liam curiously.

'You could go down it, and maybe find what's in there, you know,' suggested Fenton.

'I will!' said Liam as he flew down to the ground. He hopped in and then disappeared. After five minutes they heard a screech;

'Ahhhhhh! Oh! Huh? You-you scared me Muffin,' they heard Liam say. When Bella heard the word "Muffin" she went nuts;

'Oh! Oh! Muffin are you down there? I'm coming down too!' said Bella as she dived down.

Bella you're not gonna fit!' yelled Fenton. 'Liam will come up with Muffin. Calm down. Deep breaths, deep breaths,' said Fenton calmly. Bella got back up and looked down at the hole impatiently. Soon Liam came up with Muffin;

'Muffin, is that you?' said Custard in disbelief.

'What does it look like?' laughed Muffin. He got up and hugged the others.

'How did you get down there, Muffin?' asked Bella curiously.

'Well,' started Muffin. 'It all began when I blew away, I crashed into the water and a big squid saw me and wrapped me in its long wriggly hand thing-'

'It's called a tentacle,' said Custard shortly.

'-anyway, it was swimming along and then a big shark ate the squid and I swam through the water as fast as I could. I looked up and saw an island not too far away so I swam to it and then a mole grabbed me and carried me underground and then that's where you found me,' explained Muffin. The others oohed and ahhed.

'Also, umm, Rex came in and mixed a potion, became you and then pretended to be you,' said Liam.

'What? How could he?' cried Muffin.

'Now, we have a gem to find!' said Fenton.

'Glad you are back,' he whispered to Muffin. Muffin smiled. After hours of searching they heard footsteps nearby.

'Oh no! Not the man and the hounds again!' cried Bella. But it wasn't the man and the hounds. To their surprise it was the fake Muffin.

'Well hello. I see you've found Muffin here. Did you find the gem?' he said, a slight smile on his face. Fenton shook his head.

'Aha! I knew you wouldn't find it! And guess why you didn't find Maclin Island?' he said.

'Why?' said Fenton.

'Because it doesn't exist!' he sneered. The others sighed miserably.

'I tried to lead you off the trail, and it worked! All I need to do is find the gem and give it to my master and I'll have whatever I want!' he cheered. Muffin glared at him. He hated him so much that he ran and attempted to pounce on Rex but failed because Rex did something extraordinary, he shape-shifted into an elephant and stood there watching Muffin attempt to attack him. He laughed at Muffin and turned into a big black tarantula, that was what Muffin was most scared of. He shrieked and then Fenton jumped and pushed Muffin aside to save him. Muffin gave a sigh of relief.

'Thank you,' he said. 'That was a close one!' 'Yeah, you're welcome.'

'I know just what to do!' said Liam cunningly. Liam and Bella sprang on Rex and bit and pecked him.

'GET OFF ME YOU RABID PACK ANIMAL!', shrieked Rex. Liam flew off Rex while Bella did it again. She threw Rex up in the air and when he came crashing down she let him sniff her tail so he sprang away because Rex is allergic to horse hairs. He hurtled away off the island and crashed into the sea.

'Bye, bye!' giggled Muffin. The others laughed.

'Now, how are we going to find the gem now, since Maclin Island doesn't exist?' asked Liam cautiously.

'We'll see. But first we need to get to the cruiser.' said Fenton. And without another word they all went back to the cruiser. They were all happy to have the real Muffin back.

Oh, it is so lovely to have you back, Muffin!' said Bella joyfully.

'Yeah, we all really missed you!' added Liam. Custard smiled at Muffin and said; 'Adventure awaits!' Muffin smiled back.

'Good to have you back, buddie!' said a delighted voice that belonged to Fenton. Soon, they were all relaxed in the cruiser with only one thing to think about, how were they getting the gem now?!

'I think I know where to go,' stated Liam. The others looked at him in excitement. 'It's nowhere nice, it's an awfully terrible place, so it is. It's called The Isle of Tragedy. It's one of the scariest places on Earth! The gem is there because it is native to the island. I think it's kept in The Chamber Of Doom. I'm not sure but I think it is because it's the most highly guarded place on the Isle.' The others gave him terrified looks. Bella opened her mouth but nothing came out.

'Have you bit your tongue?' giggled Custard looking at the horse.

'No!' she said.

'And how exactly do we get to the Isle Of Magic?' said Custard, looking at Liam in great interest.

'It's the Isle of Tragedy,' (Custard rolled his eyes) 'also we get there by boat and it will probably take about three days to get there and-'

'THREE DAYS!' shrieked Custard.

'Yes, three days, that's what I said,' said Liam. 'Oh, Custard, the days will go by quicker than you ever expected. You won't even notice,' said Liam, staring at Custard's eyes.

'Aren't we supposed to get there as quickly as we can?' asked Custard.

'Yes but that is the quickest way unless we were travelling at the speed of light!' laughed Liam. Custard huffed and puffed until the others soothed him. They grabbed some cucumbers and mashed up bananas from the snack bar. They put the cucumbers on his eyes and the mush on his face.

'This is nice,' said Custard. 'I can't wait to take it off and have a nice clean and scented face.' The others stared at each other in surprise and they realised that they had forgotten about how to take it off! They thought of an excuse to leave as fast as they could;

'We uhh, have to go to the uhh, snack bar! To uhh, get some more fruit for your uhh, wonderful face!'said the others quickly. Custard was getting suspicious. A few hours later they were all a little bit tired from the journey around the small island.

Custard was calling on the others to clean his face but he couldn't find them. He went into the snack bar and looked in a nearby mirror and screamed; 'HOW DARE THEY PUT MUSHY FOOD ON MY FACE WITHOUT THINKING HOW TO CLEAN IT OFF!' he roared. The others heard him and made a run for it, they all ran to the lounges on the third floor. Custard came as well but he couldn't see them. The others made a decision very quickly and did it. They all dived into the water with a loud splash! Custard looked down at them and then he was not thinking because he leant over the barrier too far and splash! He landed back first into the water. They were all very surprised because Custard usually tried to stay away from the sea water but they knew where this was going! Custard dipped his face under the water and then all the mush on his face cleared off of his face and into the water, he saw all this cream-coloured mush travel through the water in the opposite direction. The others could see Custard's head bob up and down in the water.

'I'm free, I'm free!' they heard Custard say. It was hard to hear because his mouth was full of water and their ears were full of water. They all climbed up the water slide and dried themselves by giving themselves a big shake all over. Afterwards, they all went to bed so they could be up early in the morning.

Chapter 6.

The sun shone on their faces in the early morning. They all woke at almost the same time. It was quite a nice morning, the sky was almost clear and there was only a slight breeze. They were all excited for breakfast, all the swimming the night before had made them hungry and tired. They discussed their journey while they ate. After breakfast they all went to the lounges on the top floor but, just then Fenton stopped them;

'We can't have the same incident as last time,' he began. 'Muffin and Liam, you two go down to the beds so neither of you blow away. Bella, Custard, you're with me-' (Bella glared at Custard and followed Fenton) '-Bella, you're a strong swimmer-' (Bella nodded) '-can you somehow get off the twigs and seaweed from the side because it's all blowing around the boat and interacting with the propeller, mhm! Try the other side too. And then call up to us and then we'll stop the boat and you can help get the stuff off of the propeller. Bella agreed to the plan, she went down to the water about ten minutes later.

'What am I going to do?' asked Custard curiously.

'You're with me, Custard, and you're going to help me with steering, accelerating and slowing down the cruiser.'

'Oh, pressing buttons, it can't be all bad, can it?' Thought Custard to himself. Fenton and Custard went up to the boat's control station, it was on the fourth floor, access was placed in the middle of the third floor, it was just a little bit higher and it had a small ramp from the third floor leading up to it. They walked up the ramp and Fenton took charge;

'Ok, Custard, you sit there and then I will sit- Custard, hello, is anyone in there?!' (Custard was staring at the floor and then jumped and looked at Fenton when he spoke) 'Anyway, as I was saying, I am going to sit here. When you get into your seat I want you to take that megaphone and shout through it as loud as you can! Now read this piece of paper and yell into the megaphone, ok?' Custard read the piece of paper which said; na na ca ca sa sa ha ha. Custard stared at him in disbelief and embarrassment and said;

'Seriously, why can't you?' he said.

'Because I am a little bit busy,' said Fenton as he got out a tool-kit. Custard took the megaphone reluctantly and yelled at the top of his voice;

'NA NA CA CA SA SA HA HA!' he coughed and then said; 'Why, why?!' he spluttered. Down below Bella had heard the sign and started to get cleaning the sides of the cruiser. Soon, she swam up and said to stop the boat so that she could clean the propeller. Later, she finished cleaning and climbed back onto the boat. She went to the bathroom and dried herself with a clean towel. Fenton said that Custard could sunbathe now and he could steer the cruiser on his own now. Custard bolted to the bathroom to wash his paws and had to wash them in the water instead because the bathroom was occupied. When he finished washing his paws he went up to the third floor to sunbathe. Liam came up to Fenton with a map and said;

Here's the map to the Isle of Tragedy, just follow along and oh, here's Korry Island!' Liam pointed to an island called Korry Island on the map and then pointed to the real island. Soon, it was dinner-time, they were all very tired so they ate and yawned at the same time. After they finished eating they all went straight to bed.

Chapter 7.

The next morning was very dull and cloudy. Nothing seemed to be bright or colourful, it all just seemed colourless and spooky. Muffin was up first because he wanted to have breakfast early. The others awoke a little while later and then came down to the snack bar apart from Custard who of course was doing his daily wash. They all had some bread and butter for breakfast much to Liam's delight, but Muffin wanted marshmallows for breakfast instead! Bella asked Liam how long it would take to get to the island, Liam said it would take about a day and a half.

They were all destined to get The Gem Of Destiny to save Muffin. Fenton steered the cruiser and came to a big big rock;

'How're we supposed to get past here?' said Liam.

'I'm not sure,' said Fenton as he scratched his head.

'Ugh, what's all this?! It's wasting my special sunbathing time! Make it QUICK!' complained Custard.

'Oh Custard, all you do is lay on a pillow and get burnt in the sun,' began Muffin, indignantly. Custard rolled his eyes and looked back at Fenton.

'It's just these rocks I-I can't get past them,' he said.

'Oh no!' began Custard, sarcastically. 'Is it really that big of a deal?' he said. The others glared at him and said;

'We need to get to the Isle of Trage-' 'Yeah, yeah the Isle of so and so, we need to get to,' he finished. The others rolled their eyes and whispered; 'Ugh, typical Custard.' They all thought hard until an idea struck Fenton's head;

'I've got it! All we need to do is get the boat around Catty Cakes Island and then we are past the rocks!' he cried happily.

'Awesome!' sighed Liam happily.

'Brilliant!' said Bella, joyfully.

'Yippee!' said Muffin as he jumped about gleefully.

'Here, umm, I'll go and get some rope while you guys stay here.' said Fenton as he charged down the ramp. The others were so excited until, suddenly, dark clouds were forming in the sky, they heard thunder rumbling under their feet. A sliver of cold air prickled their noses and sent a big shiver down their spines. They all stood there, frozen with fear of what was coming.

The wind rippled their ears and prickled their lips which were tightly shut. They still stood completely still, not moving a muscle. Dark shapes were coming out of the water, instead of growling they were squeaking in a very uncomfortable way which unfortunately was even more terrifying. They had the teeth of sharks, the claws of bears, the eyes of pythons, and the tail of a dinosaur. They wondered what it could be. Was it a dinosaur, was it a sea-monster, was it just that they might be dreaming? But they didn't know. It bashed into the side of the boat, leaving a big black mark, all these black bubbles started to form around its mouth. Finally, Muffin pointed out that they needed to do something;

'Guys, come on, we need to get Fenton to drive away!' The others came back to life and nodded. Bella and Liam ran off to get Fenton. Poor Custard was hiding under the unit, he was petrified. Soon, the others came with Fenton who was sweating all over, for he was very hot from all the work even though it was freezing outside. Fenton jumped in the main chair and said;

'This may be a bumpy ride, so hold on!'

'WAIT!' cried Custard. Everyone stopped and looked at him in panicked faces. 'Can we huddle in the beds?' he asked, a cheeky smile forming in his face.

'Ok,' said Fenton. 'Just, hold on and you only have ten seconds to go down so hurry!' The others rushed down the ramp and down the stairs to the beds, it felt much more cosy to them. Muffin huddled into one of the blankets and so did the others. Their cheeks squished against each other. They were all quivering in fear. A big bang was heard, they all jumped in fear. And then, they saw that they were moving, they could see the landscape out of the window which was moving. It was getting very dark, the clouds were closing in on them and the night was getting nearer. They heard a cheer of joy so they all walked cautiously up the stairs and ramp and found Fenton smiling.

'They're away!' he cried with glee. The others celebrated with him. He was still steering the boat though. They only had two days to save Muffin! They couldn't afford to lose any more time. The boat sped through the water, avoiding waves coming and going. They created some waves behind them but they didn't notice. It was nearly eight o'clock when they finally stopped! They were very hungry for supper since they hadn't had anything since lunch. They ate well and discussed all sorts of things they would do when they got to the island;

'I know! We could go to human university and get educated to become professional spies and come back here and take em' out!' suggested Liam.

'Or,' began Fenton. 'We could come there tomorrow and hide from them.' Everyone nodded. They cleared up their mess and went straight to bed;

'Good night!' said Muffin, tiredly.

'Night,' sighed Custard as he closed his eyes. Soon, only one was up, and that was Liam. He was the only one that wasn't tired. He watched the others sleep peacefully. He wanted to go outside even though it was dark. He silently flew out of the room, not daring to make a sound, for he did not want to disturb the others or anything else. Click, click, click! Click, click, click! There seemed to be a clicking noise going on. Liam heard it, he wanted to go and see what it was as fast as he could but he didn't want to run in case he distubed the others. He tiptoed up to the third floor and went up the left way because he knew that going up the right way had lots of creaky floor boards but the left only had a few. He soon got around to the loungers and ducked under them to have a look. He soon saw what was making the noise, a wild woodpecker was hitting its beak onto the cruiser and that's what was making the click sound. He stood there to watch it and then it flew away. Liam flew up onto the tip of the cruiser to have a look at the sea. You couldn't really see anything because it was dark but Liam was good at seeing things in the dark because he ate a lot of carrots and had excellent night vision. He decided to go back into the warm cruiser and snuggle with the others. So, he went into bed, not a sound was made, all was quiet.

Chapter 8.

They all woke with a jump by hearing a bang that sounded familiar. It was the bang from when Fenton was steering the boat away from the monsters! They were all a little bit confused though, why would Fenton be up this early? They all lifted up the covers on Fenton's bed and found a bunch of pillows! Did someone kidnap him? Some of them thought and others thought that he had turned into a pillow himself! Well, gladly none of that happened, it was just Fenton getting up early and getting the cruiser started and putting pillows on his bed. So, don't worry, he is safe! The others bolted to the fourth floor and sure enough found Fenton steering the boat, he looked quite neat compared to them since they were a mess.

'Oh, hello,' said Fenton politely.

'Oh, Fenton, you made us worried sick!' cried Bella.

'Oh, sorry, didn't mean to worry you in any way.' said Fenton with a frown. The others nodded and said;

Why are you up so early?' they said together.

'I needed to get a head start on getting the gem,' he said.

'Ok.' Muffin started to giggle. The others stared at him in surprise.

'Why are you giggling, what's so funny?' asked Custard cautiously. Muffin pointed at Custard's leg and to their surprise there was a pair of dirty pants stuck on his legs. Custard looked at it, he was speechless, they could see the look of horror on his face. He finally let out a noise but instead of actual words he let out a shriek. The others giggled to see their friend running around mad this early in the morning. He ran to the bathroom, shut the door and started to wash himself very quickly because he was very embarrassed. Later he came back up looking very clean. He watched the others stare at him and then he stood up strongly and puffed his chest out to look brave. He got the opposite reaction of what he was expecting, instead of an oohh or an ahh he got ha ha ha! He stood there looking displeased;'

'Why're you laughing?' he said, his chest sinking slightly.

'You're being funny!' giggled Muffin. Custard needed to giggle as well so to the others surprise he started to laugh at himself! The others chimed in and had some fun. Fenton was still driving the boat, he was looking left and right constantly. Everyone focused their attention on Fenton;

'You ok, Fen?' asked Custard cautiously. Fenton nodded and said;

'Yes, it's just that the island could be anywhere so we need to have a good look so we don't miss it.' The others nodded and ran around the cruiser to different viewpoints to see the island. It was almost eleven o'clock, they were getting hungry so they took turns to have lunch, two of them had lunch at a time and then when they'd finished they went back to looking around. They had had quite a yummy lunch, toast, cereal, fruit and vegetables, they all enjoyed it very much. No one wanted to go back to work but unfortunately, they had to. Finally, Liam said that they didn't need to be on the lookout because they could follow the map instead. Everyone agreed to Liam's suggestion. Soon, they were all just chilling out, but it was too hot for them so a few of them sat on the open edge of the cruiser and dipped their feet into the cold water. It was a lovely afternoon but Fenton didn't take not even one break while he was driving the boat. He was determined to find the Gem of Destiny before midnight. It was one o'clock and they had arrived at Silly Seas. Silly Seas was a sea that went all the way to Bobby Bottoms Bay! But Silly Seas also leads to the River of Red which is a river just outside of the Isle of Tragedy. This was a great help to them. They had a quick snack and went back to sunbathing and swimming. Suddenly, a big cave appeared round a corner, blocking the way, you couldn't get past it unless you could fly! Well, only Liam could fly but the others couldn't, what were they going to do?

'Huh?!' gasped Liam.

'What?!' the others said together.

'I know what this is! This is the Cave of Catastrophe!' said Liam. Custard frowned and said;

'What do we know about this cave, I mean it's blocking the way!?' said Custard, gloomily.

'I have been in this cave before and it's not that bad,' said Liam as he stared into the infinite darkness of the cave. Liam knew how to get past it but he was on his own that time. He thought hard and then began to click his claws and flap his wings. Soon, he had an idea;

'We need to go into the cave and come out the other way.' Custard frowned;

'You mean that we have to go in there and go out of it on the other end?' he said. The others nodded. They drove the cruiser into the dark cave. They heard drips of water pour down the cave walls. The cave rumbled once or twice a minute, it was like it was talking to them. Now and again a small rock fell from the roof and made a big splash in the water. It was quite interesting to be in a big cave that was very cool. The cave was so fascinating to them apart from Custard who disliked the cave very much. He shivered all the way through the cave, chattering his teeth and shaking all over. The cave was full of interesting insects such as the boulder beetle, secret spider, fuzzy fly and the drum dragonfly. Soon, they came to a small hole of sunlight in the wall of the cave, it could only fit one person through it, maximum. Everyone could get through easily except for Bella. Custard went first, then Liam and then Muffin. Fenton stayed behind with Bella so he could tell her his ideas;

'Now, what you have to do if you want to get through the hole in one piece, is that you stretch out your legs and try and be as long as you can so that you can fit most of your body through the hole and then we'll do the rest.' Fenton went behind Bella and waited for her to go through the hole. Bella stood next to the hole, thinking what to do and then what Fenton said came into her mind;

'Stretch out your legs and we'll do the rest,' she thought. She reared up onto her hind-legs, she curled in her front legs so she could fall forward and stretch them out to catch her in the hole of the cave. Bella positioned herself precisely and then with a splash in the water she went, she fell forward only for a millisecond and as quick as a flash she sprang out her front-legs and they hooked onto the other side of the hole as she lifted up her hind legs so she could try and jump through the hole. Sooner or later she got most of her body through the hole leaving just her hind legs and her fluffy tail. The others grabbed Bella's front legs and pulled, Fenton caught her hind legs and pushed, soon Bella only had her ankles and hoofs to go but it was getting too breathtaking for them, they'd been doing this for forty minutes so they were all worn-out. Fenton took a deep breath and pushed as hard as he could, Bella squirmed because she was so tired of being stuck in a hole for forty minutes. Fenton only had her hoofs left before the others started to help. They finally got Bella out of the hole. Fenton sprang through the hole after Bella slid out.

'Well, that was fun.' said Custard sarcastically.

'More like tiring,' squeaked Muffin. I need a rest.'

'Me too, I am so tired,' said Liam. 'Are you ok Bella?' Bella nodded as she stretched her legs and neck.

'Me three,' added Custard.

'Me-' '-all of us do!' finished Bella.

'Umm, I'm not sure if you've noticed but there is a slight problem,' Custard whispered to them, (The others paused and looked at him with worried expressions on their faces)

'Where is the cruiser?' The others threw startled looks at each other, they'd forgotten about the cruiser!

'Uhh, stupid me, I should've flew back and steered the cruiser round the cave!' wailed Liam.

'Liam, it's not your fault, it's all of our faults!' assured Fenton.

'You mean it's all your faults not mine, I mean I'm a hero!' bragged Custard. The others rolled their eyes. All their attention went straight back to Liam. Liam looked up and nodded.

'Go through the hole and zoom to the cruiser and steer it around the cave, there's still time!' cried Bella. Liam launched himself through the hole and they heard the rapid flaps of his wings as he bolted through the cave. Soon they saw a very white boat come through the water and around the jaggy and sharp rocks. They all cheered with excitement and jumped around in the shimmering blue water. Once or twice Liam had to stop and look down at the water to see where some of the rocks were under the water. Finally, he reached them, they all scrambled onto the boat and rushed to the loungers on the second floor and wrapped up nice and cosy to get some warmth because the water was very cold and the cold air nipped their lips. They huddled into the beds, it wasn't even eleven o'clock yet!

Chapter 9.

When the time reached one o'clock everyone was so tired that they had even forgotten about their lunch until Muffin complained that his tummy hurted;

'Oww, my tummy hurts! Oww,' wailed Muffin. 'It is rumbling like crazy, what's wrong with it?!'

'You're just hungry, that's all-wait,' (The others looked at Liam in surprise) 'We haven't had our lunch yet!' The others looked up and instead of worried or surprised looks they smiled.

'YAY!' cheered Bella. 'I am so glad we haven't because I thought we did, so I thought I couldn't have anything else to eat!' They all rushed to the snack bar, it sounded like a herd of elephants playing tig. They had a delicious lunch: Sausages, ham, eggs, fruit, bread and butter, milk and some pancakes. They gobbled it up in a minute, leaving some for Fenton to have.

'I'll go up and steer while Fenton has his lunch,' said Liam.

'Muffin make sure to leave some of that toast too!' Muffin put down the piece of toast he was going to eat and giggled. Liam went up the small set of stairs up the other set of stairs and up the ramp to where Fenton was.

'Hi, umm thought you'd like your lunch so I'll steer and you can go and eat your lunch.'

'Thanks, I kinda needed a break and lunch.' Fenton went down the ramp leaving Liam to steer. Thirty minutes later Fenton came up the ramp and said that he would steer again,

Liam nodded and headed down the ramp and sat on the loungers and watched the smooth glittering water fade away. Later, they were all out playing, splashing in the water, playing hide and seek around the boat, pretending that they had magical powers, all was good. By five o'clock the sun was starting to lower itself in the sky. This told them that they had until the sun set completely to save Muffin. Later, they saw a tall black mountain with red sparkling on it. It was very thin but tall. At the bottom of it there was a small entrance that went underground and was guarded by these demon things that held glowing red staffs. There was a big palace but it didn't look like a palace, it looked like a dungeon. It was black and red with a thousand demons holding staffs and even some holding swords. They somehow had to sneak in without being seen or caught.

'How can we not be seen there's like a million of them!?' moaned Custard.

'Maybe we can get seen but we can't be caught,' said Fenton thoughtfully.

'Look! There's the River of Red!' said Bella.

'What use does that make to us?!' snapped Custard. Bella scowled at him.

'I think we need to disguise ourself.'

'To disguise ourself to look like one of them!' said Liam.

'Exactly!' said Fenton.

'But how?' asked Custard.

'There's make-up in the bathroom, maybe we can use some make-up!' cried Bella. They all agreed and ran down to the bathroom. Luckily, there was a lot of red and black. There was also paint in the bathroom so they used paint as well. Bella painted the orange on Fenton red, she painted all the white black and then the tiny details red. Liam's yellow tummy got painted black with some fiery red stripes on it, his beak and face were mainly black but with a little bit of red. His black feathers stayed black. Muffin was painted black but with tiny red outlines of his eyes and mouth, his little muffin liner was red with black stripes down the crinkles. Bella was painted mostly black leaving her mane, tail, hoofs and face. Her mane and tail were red with a few black stripes down them. Her hooves were red, her eyes, mouth, nose and the inside of her ears were red too. Custard was black with small red dots and stripes on him. They were ready. Before they went Bella made a red and black lead for Muffin so that he was a pet. Muffin went on all fours so he looked like a demon dog pet. Fenton had the leash in his paw so that he could talk without having to take a leash out of his mouth. They came to the entrance of the island, there were two demon guards standing at the entrance;

'Ticket?' said one of the guards. They looked at each other and made up an excuse;

'Ticket yes yes, hmm, Lava! Bad Lava very bad Lava, why did you eat the tickets!? Now we can't come to the island!' cried Bella in a very ladyish voice. Muffin squeaked sadly.

'Ugh, c'mon I guess we have to go.'

'Wait!' cried one of the guards. Bella smiled as she stopped.

'Yes?' she said excitedly.

'You can come in, here.' (He handed her five tickets)

'Oh thank you.' she said with a deep smile growing on her face.

'My pleasure.' said the guard. They walked in taking deep breaths thinking that that was a close one. They took in everything around them, it was all very dull and black. Liam looked at the entrance just before the mountain;

'That's the entrance to the Chamber Of Doom. The gem is somewhere in it.' 'So we need to find it!' said Bella bravely.

'But how can we get in there? I mean it's guarded by tons of guards!' said Custard dully.

'Good point,' said Fenton. 'We could dress up as them!' suggested Muffin.

'Great idea!' complemented Liam.

'No not dressing up again!' moaned Custard.

'Oh if you don't want to, you can stay here all alone!' said Bella dramatically.

'Ugh, fine!' wailed Custard. They bolted to their boat and got changed as quickly as they could.

'How do I look?' asked Bella cautiously.

'Umm, lovely!' lied Custard.

'Umm Fenton what do you think, do I look like those demon guards?' said Bella as she looked over at Fenton. Fenton looked at her and said;

'Close enough!'

'Anyways let's get going!' said Liam. Instead Bella added paper spikes to the leash and made Muffin a paper spiked collar. 'Are we all ready?' asked Liam.

'Wait!' called Bella. The others stared at her in surprise. Bella placed a spiked chain around her neck and added a little more make-up to her face so that nobody could see her eyelashes.

'Ready!' she said in a low tone. The others stared at her in a why-are-you-talking-in-a-very-low-voice way.

'I am meant to be a boy!' she said.

'Maybe just don't talk unless someone asks you a question and practise it!' suggested Liam. They all nodded and ran off the cruiser and back onto the island. They showed the tickets and went through the entrance. They came to the other entrance and walked through it but unfortunately they were stopped;

'And where do you think you're going-'

'Oh we are just going down to guard deeper!' said Liam quickly.

'I wasn't finished,' continued the guard, 'I was saying where do you think you're going without a staff?' and handed Bella, Liam, Custard and Fenton a staff.

'Thank you,' said Fenton, relieved, 'someone stole ours!' The guard nodded and let them through.

'That was a close one!' whispered Fenton.

'Yeah, we would've been burned!' added Liam. They tiptoed through the passage, it was getting darker and darker the more they went down the tunnel. It got thinner and thinner, it was like the walls were closing in on them. Luckily, there were some torches lit on the walls so they could see. The tunnel echoed whatever they said;

'This is going on forever!' complained Custard. Is going on forever, going on forever, on forever! the echo said back. Muffin shivered and clutched Fenton's leg tightly. They soon came to another entrance that was guarded by what looked like Anubis, the God of the Underworld. They stared at it and walked past it casually, but before they even got a metre away from it it stopped them and said; 'WHO GOES THERE!?'

'Oh umm we are-'

'They won't hear you Liam, you have to shout,' said Fenton.

'Go on.' Liam yelled at the Anubis with all his might; 'WE ARE THE DEMON GUARDS, WE HAVE PERMISSION TO GUARD DEEPER SO LET US THROUGH! I COMMAND YOU!!!' The Anubis nodded and let them through. Soon they came to an entrance guarded by six demon guards, they let them through of course. Later, they came to another entrance which said The Chamber Of Doom on it, this was the entrance to The Chamber of Doom. Inside the chamber were no other than twenty-five Anubi! They stood still watching them enter. Fenton thought hard; How are we going to get the gem with all these Anubi about? he thought. He needed something to make a distraction.

'Custard, can you make a distraction to distract all these Anubi?' asked Fenton desperately.

'Sure thing,' said Custard. 'I'll dance and cause trouble!' He trotted off and disappeared through the entrance and in the tunnel.

'Hope this works!' said Fenton. Bella ran after Custard for some reason. They heard her say something which sounded like this;

'Here use this and play track three, ok?' Then they heard an 'ok'. Bella ran back and watched. Custard stood in the entrance and had what looked like a boombox. He fiddled with the buttons until a very poppy track played. Custard danced in a very interesting and uncomfortable way and even sang;

'Take me home come on you sheepish guards. Come with me on my world tour! I don't take any regards! You kinda weird, you are so sour! I hate that you can't go around and prowl!' The Anubi glared at him and raised their staffs and chased after Custard. Still carrying the boombox with him he turned it up even louder to make the Anubi even more angry. Soon he had all the guards in the passage up and running out of the entrance and around the island. He snuck back in and ran down to the others very proud of himself indeed.

'Well done Custard!' they all said together.

'That was great!' added Bella.

'Nice work!' complemented Liam. They all stood looking around for the gem. All there was was a mark on one of the tiles on the floor and nothing else. Bella stood on the tile and then the tile fell down making Bella plummet with it all the way down. The others stared after her in shock and panic apart from Fenton;

'Good old Bella, she found us the way! We need to stand on the tile and it'll take us underground to the gem!' The others nodded and they all took turns on going on the tile, when they landed they landed on a silver slab in the middle of what looked like lava. 'LAVA! THIS IS TOO MUCH!' shrieked Custard as he clutched Fenton. Fenton broke off a chunk from the boombox and dipped it into the lava which surprisingly did not dissolve or burn. He dipped his leg in and nothing happened all it was was coloured water, nothing else. He told the others that it was safe so they all swam across the coloured water and onto some more slabs but this time they were gold not silver. In the middle of it was The Gem Of Destiny being held on a small stone pillar. They all cheered with glee. Fenton said not to touch it in case it was booby trapped. He walked around the pillar that was holding the gem up and then said that it was ok, they took the gem and to their greatest relief nothing happened, the walls didn't fall down they didn't get captured or anything bad but the main thing is that they finally got The Gem Of Destiny! They all gathered around it and touched it. Everyone said this apart from Muffin;

'Our wish for this century and our whole entire life is that our friend Muffin will live with us as long as we live!' Nothing happened.

'Maybe we need to shake it or say it more clearly!' suggested Custard. They shook it and said it more clearly but it didn't work.

'Why isn't it working? Maybe someone else has already made a wish!' sighed Liam. They tried two more times but nothing. Fenton walked around the small area and saw a familiar marking on the wall and pressed it, nothing happened. He got the others to help him but when they helped it sucked them all down a hole and onto a crystal slab, this time not surrounded by anything all that was there was a light blue gem in the middle. They ran to it and picked it up but this time the rocks rumbled, rocks were falling down, the walls were collapsing! Bella grabbed a heavy rock and banged it against the rocky wall and a small glimpse of light started shining through it. They all started bashing rocks against the walls and soon the hole got bigger and bigger and light flooded into the cave. They squeezed through the hole with Fenton carrying the gem of Destiny. They appeared at the edge of the island with a whole lot of guards and Anubi running after them, they hopped into their boat and sped away. They stopped the cruiser when they were far away enough from the Isle Of Tragedy. They all went to the loungers on the third floor and held the Gem Of Destiny up high. They all held onto it and said;

'Our wish for this century and our whole entire life is that our friend Muffin will live with us as long as we live!' Blue sparkles started to surround the gem and it flew out of their clutches. A beautiful, glowing beam of blue shimmery light travelled down from the sky into the gem and then down into Muffin. Muffin began to lift up into the sky and float surrounded by blue light and then he lightly lowered himself down and landed on the ground. He celebrated with the others;

'Yay, Muffin! You're with us forever!' cheered Bella.

'I am glad you're not gone!' said Liam. They all hugged Muffin tightly. They celebrated for a little while until Custard pointed out something;

'There's just one problem, how're we gonna get home?' They all exchanged looks at each other. They went in the cruiser and back to the mainland to where Custard lived.

'Since you guys don't really have a proper home, want to stay at my place?' said Custard with a smile on his face. The other's faces brightened up. They were staying at Custard's house! They loved their new life but before Custard's owner came home Bella made them all collars that said their names on them. When Custard's owner came home she was so surprised to see not just Custard but another four creatures in her house. She accepted it because Muffin told her about the adventure they had had and all their names so she agreed to take care of them. Luckily, Custard wasn't scared to speak human language in front of his owner any more so they all talked in a way that everyone understood them.

They were all very happy to live where they lived and have what they had. A great friendship.

They were all now ready for their next adventure!